T0380287

The Baby
in the
Hay

and Other Christmas Thoughts

Nancy L. Miller

WESTBOW
P R E S S®
A DIVISION OF THOMAS NELSON
& ZONDERVAN

WestBow Press books may be ordered through
booksellers or by contacting:

WestBow Press
A Division of Thomas Nelson & Zondervan
1663 Liberty Drive
Bloomington, IN 47403
www.westbowpress.com
844-714-3454

Scriptures are taken from King James version of the Bible, public domain.

ISBN: 979-8-3850-2466-7 (sc)
ISBN: 979-8-3850-2467-4 (e)

Library of Congress Control Number: 2024908834

Print information available on the last page.

WestBow Press rev. date: 07/11/2024

A special thank you to my dear husband, Roger, who has stayed with me through life's challenges. You always have my love. Special thanks to Kristin Trehearne-Lane, who did my first read and edit. She helped immensely. And thank you to my special prayer partners. Much love and appreciation!

Above all, I thank God the Father who sent His Son to become the real baby in the hay.

Contents

The Baby in the Hay 1

Crooked Foot 28

The Offering 41

He Came for Us 50

This Tiny Human Baby's Hand 51

Simple Thoughts 52

Christmas Bird 53

Christmas Rush 54

Did You See the Baby? 55

He Lives—Eternal King! 56

In the Midst of Christmas Parties 57

Christmas in Unsettled Times 58

Let Us Rediscover Christmas 59

About the Author 61

The Baby in the Hay

The crisp November air danced with dried oak leaves above the crumbling sidewalk. The clear azure sky enhanced Marcus's eyes as he stared longingly at the train disappearing into the tunnel.

Mr. Robinson's froggy voice vibrated through the hobby store's window. "Go home, Marcus. You've been here half an hour; your mom will be worried."

Marcus took one more long look as the train appeared from the other side of the mountain and buzzed past miniature houses and ant-sized people. Its streamlined silver body was beautiful in the eleven-year-old's eyes.

Last summer, Marcus and his dad saw the train as soon as Mr. Robinson set it up. They came often to this store, famous in this county for its train sets.

"Marcus," Dad had said, "if you do more chores at home, this could be your Christmas present from Mom and me this year."

But everything had changed since Dad said that, and Marcus was doing most of the chores now.

Marcus pulled at the collar of his oversized coat. Mom told him that Cousin Jeff's coat would fit perfectly later, but why did he have to wear a used coat this winter anyway? He got a new coat every year before this one. He turned and ran out of Mr. Robinson's sight, leaving his dream train in the window.

NANCY L. MILLER

Marcus ran hard and fast, tears filling his eyes.

"Why did Dad have to die?" he shouted angrily into the chilly air.

He ran over to the next street then down beside the railroad track and followed it into the loading dock area of the old glass factory.

Discarded chunks of previously molten glass were mixed with gravel on the ground. The dark-green, black, red and orange glass rocks were collected by all the kids in the neighborhood. Only the pebble-sized glass pieces were left. Marcus ducked his head and found his hiding place under the last dock. Weeds grew tall between the loading dock platforms and the overhangs, making a secluded clubhouse effect. Mom was going to the store after work today so she wouldn't be home yet anyway. He would stay here until his tears dried. Aunt Lynn would be home busy with Gracie, and they would be too busy to miss him.

In the last few months, Marcus came here to cry alone. He was too big to cry like his little sister, but he was too young to cry quietly like he'd seen his dad cry at Grandpa's funeral. No one could see his tears here except the neighborhood cat. The feline wandered in and bumped up against Marcus's leg. Marcus considered him a friend. They could just hang out together, and the cat couldn't give him instructions.

Since Dad died, Mom was always sad or working and Aunt Lynn was at his house cooking and giving orders. Besides, his little sister, Gracie, was too young to play with him and was always messing up his train set. Marcus felt alone and frustrated. He felt cheated that his father was gone.

Marcus poked a stick in the gravel and began drawing aimlessly. A lump grew in his throat as his mind wandered

2

back to August. He could see the policeman at their front door. He remembered the words "terrible accident" and "semi." He could see Mom's fear as she and the kids left quickly to drive to the hospital in the next county. Marcus could see Dad with closed eyes and tubes in his throat and nose. He could see the fluctuating lines and graphs of the machines plugged into Dad. Then he remembered it seemed like forever that they visited Dad this way, until the day the doctor met them in the hall.

"We need to talk, Mrs. Hammond," the doctor said.

After they said their goodbyes to Dad, the doctors turned off all the machines. That night, Dad was gone. Dad had been in the hospital for weeks, never knowing, never seeing, and never hugging Marcus again. Now Dad was gone … forever.

Marcus's friend Charlie was the only one who knew Marcus came to the old glass factory. Charlie rode his bike everywhere and found Marcus there. They hung out, threw rocks at the telephone poles, and gathered glass. And today, of course, Charlie rode by.

"Marcus, your mom is looking for you!" Charlie yelled as he jumped off his bike.

"OK, I'll leave. If Mom ever found out I'm here, she'd lose it. She keeps saying strange people might hang around empty buildings."

"Why didn't you call her?" Charlie asked.

"I left my phone at home."

"I'll call her," Charlie offered, hitting the speed dial.

"Mrs. Hammond, I found Marcus. He was at my house when I came by your house," Charlie lied. "OK, I'll tell him."

"You shouldn't have lied, man. Our moms talk to each other," Marcus replied.

"No big deal. Mom went to the pharmacy," Charlie said. "Your mom said to get home now. She has to leave."

Marcus ran down the alley, past the baseball fields, then one more block to home.

"Marcus, is that you?" Marcus's mom, Marcy, yelled as she hurried to the kitchen door. She hugged and kissed Marcus in relief then scolded him in anger. "You know you're to come straight home! School's been out over an hour. Charlie said you went to his house. Why didn't you call me?" Her words flew out of her mouth faster than Marcus could answer.

"I left my phone by my bed, Mom, and I thought I could call you from Charlie's house."

"Then why didn't you call?" Mom asked.

"Well, I stopped by Mr. Robinson's, and I told Charlie to go on. I forgot, I guess."

"Oh, that train again. Marcus, we talked about that. You know now that Dad's gone I have to work two jobs to just keep up the bills. I talked to you about not having a big Christmas. Furthermore, this is the second time in two weeks I've had to look for you. You know I can't lose any more people!" Marcy got more upset the more she said. "Anyway, I've got to go to the Corner Pantry now. I changed my plans after work so that I could fix dinner and see you before I went to the next job. I'll come to kiss you good-night when I get home."

Marcus walked to his room, dropping his coat and backpack loudly on the floor.

Just then, Gracie came into the kitchen with Aunt Lynn, who lived across the hall.

"Lynn, the meat loaf and potatoes are already done. I just nuked some peas. And make sure Gracie gets to bed on time. She—*we*—didn't sleep much last night," Marcy said in a rush. "Thanks, Lynn. What would I ever do without you?"

"You know I need to do this for you guys. Where was the little doofus anyway?" asked Lynn.

"He stopped by the hobby shop again." Marcy's frustrated voice was back. "I don't know what to do with him, Lynn. Since Tim died, he's not been paying attention to anything but that silly train."

"Try to relax, Marce. Maybe you'll be busy tonight and the time will go fast. We've got things under control here."

Marcy disappeared out the kitchen door after kissing Gracie goodbye and finding Marcus in his room to kiss him.

Lynn handed plates and utensils to Gracie. "Do you remember how I showed you to set the table last week?" Lynn asked Gracie. "I need to call Uncle John. I'll get the hot food in a minute, sweetie. Marcus, wash up!" she yelled toward the bedroom.

Lynn called her husband, John, at the factory to let him know that Marcus was home and everyone was all right. John began working second shift when he and Lynn decided to house Tim's family in their own apartment building. Second shift would pay a little more, and Marcy wouldn't have to pay full price for rent. Lynn and her only sibling, Tim, were always close.

Lynn got the kids seated at the kitchen table. "Which one of you is going to say grace tonight?"

"Gracie, of course," Marcus grumbled. "It's in her name."

Gracie liked to pray so Marcus's sarcasm was wasted.

"God is great. God is good. Now we thank him for our food. Amen," Gracie said.

"That's a baby prayer," Marcus growled.

"You get to pray next time then," Lynn said, putting a generous helping of peas on Gracie's plate.

"Do I have to eat the peas?" Gracie whined.

"I think your happy mood got dragged down by a certain someone who is a grouch," Aunt Lynn said. "Eat ten peas for me and the rest of your food, then I'll decide."

Gracie piped up, "Marcus, you made Mom mad again. She thought you were lost or dead or something."

"Gracie, eat!" Lynn scolded. "I thought dinner would help us all relax. Let's just see if we can all be quiet and eat!"

Marcus picked at his food. A bite of meat loaf and baked potato and two bites of peas was all he could stomach. *I don't see why it was that big of a deal,* Marcus thought. *If Mom was sad not to see me, she could have stayed home tonight.*

"Aunt Lynn, can I be finished? I don't feel too good," Marcus said.

"Please try to eat a few more bites of meat loaf. It's your favorite," Lynn pleaded.

After ten more minutes of pushing his food around, Aunt Lynn excused Marcus.

"Why don't you take your bath before your homework tonight? It will relax you. If you get your homework done quickly, you can watch a little TV before bed."

Marcus's bath came and went, and he flung himself across his bed with his social studies book in hand. Tears welled in his eyes, and before he could clear his eyes and read one sentence, he fell asleep.

Marcy rang up a lady's pop and candy bar and hoped she wouldn't have too many more customers tonight. She had been so busy she hadn't had time to check in with Lynn. It was an hour before her shift ended, but she just needed to hear Lynn's voice.

"Hi, Lynn. How's everything?" Marcy asked.

"Well, Gracie's fine, but Marcus said he didn't feel well. I tucked him in bed since he fell asleep there. He didn't act like he had much homework."

"Lynn, I just think he's becoming more distant all the time. He doesn't seem to pay attention to anyone or anything around him anymore. I just don't know what to do," Marcy said, wanting an answer.

"It 's only been three months. We're all still in the cloudy mode. I think he'll be all right. It's gonna take time … for us all," Lynn said as positively as she could without disclosing her brokenness.

"Did Gracie go to bed OK?" Marcy inquired.

"Sure did, kid. She's your survivor. You know 'faith of a child.' God's gonna help us all, Marce. Try not to worry more than you have to. See you soon," Lynn cut off the conversation as she heard the sound of the bell on the door in Marcy's store and knew she had a customer.

When Marcy came home, Lynn greeted her with a hug. "All's quiet on the western front," Lynn said. "There's a plate for you in the fridge. You want me to pop it in the microwave for you?"

"No, I want to change clothes first," Marcy said.

"I think I hear John coming in too," Lynn replied. "Do you want me to stay, kiddo?"

7

"No, I'm fine. I'll change then relax with some TV while I eat. I won't stay up long. Thanks again, Lynn." Marcy gave her sister-in-law another hug before she let her leave.

"It will be OK," Lynn spoke gently. "Family takes care of family. We'll get through this."

As Lynn closed the door, Marcy kicked off her shoes and peaked in at each of her sleeping kids. She came back to the living room, sinking down onto the couch. She pulled her grandmother's knitted afghan snugly around her. She felt like a vacuum had sucked out all of her insides, and she wondered if she could ever feel happy again. She turned on the television to some old sit-com reruns. She thought about the wise father on the show. "Tim always did know best," she said to herself. Then she, like Marcus, cried herself to sleep.

Marcus awoke at 6:30 a.m. with cold rain prickling the window. There was a chill in the air mixed with the heavy smell of bacon frying. The television in the living room was chattering, "Today's weather is a mixed bag of cold rain changing to ice and snow. Be sure to stay tuned for more information on this winter storm watch."

Marcy came to the bedroom door. "Marcus, it's time to get up. You need to eat a good breakfast today. Aunt Lynn said you didn't eat much last night. How are you feeling?"

Marcus wasn't really sure how he felt. As soon as he realized he hadn't studied for his social studies quiz, he got a big knot in his stomach.

"Mommy, can I wear my green dress today?" Gracie asked in her perky little voice as she stood by her mom in the hall.

"Why don't you wear your brown pants and fuzzy sweater?" Marcy asked.

"The sweater itches me."

"The sweater makes you itch," Marcy corrected. "Then wear your blue sweater. I know you're just going to be with Aunt Lynn across the hall, but it's supposed to get colder today."

Gracie ran happily back to her room, while Marcus just wanted to go back to sleep. *It's just too cheerful in this house in the mornings*, he thought.

"Come on, bud," Marcy said sternly as she went back to the kitchen. "We've got to get you to school before the weather gets worse."

Marcy's other job was working in the cafeteria at Marcus's school so she always took him with her.

Moaning and wobbly, Marcus made it to the kitchen table. "I don't feel so great; I don't want any bacon," he muttered.

Marcy put her hand on Marcus's forehead. She didn't cook bacon every day, and he never turned it down when she did.

"I can't tell if you're feverish," she said as she kissed his forehead.

She went instantly in search of the thermometer. She placed it in his mouth.

"Ninety-eight point six," she said after it beeped. "I think you can go to school. If you feel worse, you can go to the nurse's office until I can take you home. Anyway, if the weather gets bad quickly, we may all leave early."

Marcus really hoped school would close. He wasn't sick but he didn't feel right, and he knew he wasn't ready for a quiz or in the mood to talk today. He shuffled into the bathroom and began brushing his teeth.

Gracie was still talkative as she came back down the hall. "Mommy, Miss Amber said we get to sing special songs for the Christmas program like last year."

9

"You do every year, dork," Marcus growled.

"Mommy, Marcus called me a dork," Gracie whined.

Marcy sent a scolding frown toward Marcus in the bathroom.

"Time to go to Aunt Lynn's, Gracie. Get your bag. We'll see you here after school."

Marcy opened the door and Gracie trotted across the hall where Aunt Lynn had just poked her head out of her door.

"Hi, Miss Sunshine! Did you have your breakfast?" Lynn closed the door and Marcy finished getting herself ready for the day.

The cold rain was not yet turning to ice, but it created a bone-chilling day. They drove to school, and although Marcus was in upper elementary school, he still had to attend creative childcare for the hour before school started.

Marcy left him in the cafeteria where the childcare group met and went into the kitchen to begin her busy day. Marcus was happy about the extra hour so that he could study, but Charlie was there and asked if Marcus got in trouble yesterday when he got home. After a brief discussion, Marcus asked Charlie about the social studies quiz since they were in the same fifth grade class. But Rusty, the childcare teacher, had a special Thanksgiving project for the whole group. Time passed too quickly, and Marcus still didn't get to study much when the bell rang.

"Charlie, my stomach hurts. Tell Miss Kennedy I'm going to tell my mom," Marcus said as Charlie was heading to class.

Marcus found his mom in the cafeteria kitchen.

"I still don't feel good, Mom," Marcus said.

"Do you think you're going to throw up?" Marcy asked.

"No, I just don't feel good," he mumbled.

Knowing Marcus's mood and the tension of the previous night, Marcy said, "Please go to class for a while and just try, Marcus."

She hugged him and sent him on his way.

Reluctantly, Marcus headed out of the cafeteria toward his classroom while Marcy got back to work.

Marcus had always been a good student, but this year was different. Miss Kennedy would be upset at Marcus. She had been pushing him all year to do better.

"I know you're smart enough, Marcus. I know you can do better," she would say. She understood his grief but thought she was doing the right thing. Marcus couldn't concentrate and wasn't self-motivated like before. He felt lost and lonely.

I don't want to go to class. I want to go home, he thought. *I've got a key. I could walk home. It won't take that long. I can get in the back door and Aunt Lynn won't even know. I'll come back after lunch and ride home with Mom. She'll think I went to class. Charlie and Miss Kennedy will think I'm with Mom or the nurse. No one will know.*

Marcus was forgetting about the rain turning to ice.

He started out into the hall. Principal Baylor had his back to Marcus at the far end of the hall, watching students go to class as they entered the building from the bus area.

As a little girl dropped her papers in front of Principal Baylor, who was helping her pick them up, Marcus saw his opportunity. He snuck back through the empty cafeteria and out the side door. He could get out, but it locked behind him. All of the cafeteria workers were at their stations in the kitchen away from the door, not seeing or hearing Marcus.

The rain was already icy, creating icicles on the shrubs. Marcus was so determined to go home that he didn't care. It wouldn't take him long. He hurried down the alley to Main Street by the Methodist church. He and his family attended there weekly before Dad died. The old, brown brick building with stained glass windows was usually a peaceful place for Marcus; Charlie's family went to church there too.

There was a wooden stable already set up for the holidays on the corner of the church yard. It contained life-size Nativity figures in it. Little icicles were forming along the roofline. The cow and donkey even had icicles on their ears.

Somewhere down Main Street, Marcus heard a siren. A police car was coming his way. Startled and not sure what to do, he jumped inside the stable and lay behind a bale of hay until the police car passed. Marcus's heart was pounding as if the police car were coming for him, but who would know he was gone this soon?

After the police car passed, Marcus looked at each of the holy family figures. They looked so serene. The Christ Child looked as if he was sleeping and warm; someone had wrapped him in real cloths. Marcus wished he could feel that relaxed and peaceful.

The church door opened, and Reverend James came out toward the mailbox as the mail truck pulled to the curb.

Marcus dove back down behind the hay.

"George, I can tell time by you. I was almost too late. Will you mail these for me?" the reverend asked the mail carrier.

"Certainly, Reverend, anything for you. It's getting slick. You'd better not stay here too long," the mail carrier replied, and then he drove on down the street.

Marcus was still trying to hide. He listened for the

footsteps to head back into the church, and then the church doors opened and closed one more time. The sleet was now turning to snow, and the ground was turning white. The snowflakes were swirling around in the stable, and they melted on the baby's eyes, making it look like he was crying. Waiting to make sure no one was near, Marcus put his head down on the hay. He thought about Mr. Robinson's shop being around the corner, but if he went there today, he could be seen. He'd better go down the alley. He hesitated.

Marcus's mind was on the train that he wanted passionately. Dad had four train sets and had them all set up in their basement. But after he died and they had to move to Aunt Lynn's apartment house, they didn't have room for the trains. Mom sold all but the smallest set. Marcus was sad, angry, and frustrated. Again, tears welled in his eyes, but he fought hard against them as he lay in the hay.

Soon he heard the baby in the hay crying, and he sat up with a start. There was an angel beside him patting the baby.

"Hush now," the angel said to Marcus. "I'm trying to get him to sleep. Mary and Joseph need their rest."

Marcus rubbed his eyes. "This must be a dream."

"Did you come to see the baby, young man?" the angel whispered. "He is your Savior."

"Well, I, I …" Marcus stammered. "I know he's my Savior, but he's not a real baby now."

"Well, what is he then?" the angel asked.

"Well, he's a man, or God, or something," Marcus replied. "He grew up, died on a cross, rose from the grave, and went to heaven."

"Well that is a very good Sunday school summary, sir, but

13

there is much more. It's a shame he had to do so much to save you humans. He must really love you people."

The angel continued. "I can come and go anywhere, and I always do what I'm told. I just wish I could feel this love you feel. Humans do strange things for love, and God himself gave up his throne to become a human because he loves you all!"

"I don't think he loves me much anymore," Marcus said with downcast eyes. "If God loved me, he wouldn't have let Dad die. I prayed, and prayed, and Dad died anyway. Then we had to sell our house and move into an apartment. It sure doesn't seem like God loves us."

"So if bad things happen, it means God doesn't love you?" the angel inquired.

"If God loved us, he would have answered our prayers," Marcus insisted.

"Maybe God did," the angel said. "What did you pray for, Marcus?"

"Hey, how do you know my name? Oh yeah, you're an angel," Marcus said. "Anyway, I prayed Dad would get well and we could have a really great Christmas."

"Well, I happen to know your dad is well now, Marcus. He's just not with you. Doesn't seem right, does it?"

"No, and I don't want to go to church, or back to school, or even home now. Everyone keeps saying they know how I feel!" Marcus was getting angry again. "Nobody knows how I feel!" Marcus was suddenly aware someone might hear him.

"He knows," the angel said calmly.

"Who knows?" Marcus was confused.

"The baby in the hay. He knows how you feel," the angel said firmly.

"How can he know? He's just a doll in the manger."

"You said yourself Jesus grew up and he's in heaven. Do you think when he was on earth he ever had friends to play with in the Judean hills? Maybe he played stick ball with them. Do you think he ever had a cold or the flu?"

"He was God," Marcus said, looking at the angel as if the angel was not making sense.

"But, the angel replied, "he was human too, so that he could understand. What happened to him when he was a teenager and a young adult, Marcus? I happen to know you grew up in this church and attended regularly until your dad died. How did Jesus feel when Joseph died?"

"I don't think the Bible says," Marcus said, perturbed. "We don't know when Joseph died."

"That's true. The Bible doesn't say, but when Jesus was dying on the cross, he asked his best friend, John, to take care of his mother, Mary. He wouldn't have done that if Joseph were around. He not only knew the pain on the cross, but somehow he knew the pain in people's broken hearts. He came to die for pain, pain of every kind. Remember when his friend Lazarus died? Jesus wept. He wept for what his friends were thinking and feeling. He loves you Marcus and wants you to know that he cares about how you feel. He will help you through this if you trust in him."

Suddenly the angel was gone and Marcus found himself in the cold reality of the Nativity scene with the winter snow whipping around him. The tears were still on the baby's eyes. But since no one was around, Marcus jumped up and ran behind the church into the alley.

Jesus wept. Jesus wept resonated in his heart. It was a joke in Sunday school to recite that verse since it was only two words. Marcus ran down the alley behind Mr. Robinson's store, crossed over Main Street, and ran down along the train track to the old glass factory. Out of breath, he jumped under one of the loading docks, sliding on the ice under the snow. As he slid, he could not catch himself, and falling hard, he hit his head on the edge of the dock. He landed unconscious under the platform. The winter storm had piled up three inches of snow by now and was continuing. Soon it would cover Marcus's footprints.

Back at school, Helen Morris, the principal's secretary, was totaling the attendance reports sent to her by all the teachers on their computers. Helen saw that Miss Kennedy reported one student already in the clinic. She yelled at the nurse in the next room. "Martha, did you forget something again?" she inquired jokingly. "You forgot to let me know Marcus Hammond is in the clinic this morning."

"Well, if he is, he's invisible! I've not seen him today!" she yelled back with a chuckle. "I'm the only one here." She spoke as she appeared at the doorway.

"Well, I'll double check with Miss Kennedy. Maybe Marcus showed up and she forgot to change the report. Thanks anyway."

Helen phoned Miss Kennedy's room.

"Hi, Brittney. Did Marcus Hammond come into class after you marked your attendance?" she asked.

"No, he never came in. Charlie said he was going to talk to his mom then go to the clinic," Miss Kennedy replied.

As soon as Helen hung up with Miss Kennedy, she rang the cafeteria.

"These kids!" she muttered under her breath. "I need to speak to Marcy Hammond please," she requested.

"Marcy, this is Helen. Is Marcus still with you? Charlie told Miss Kennedy that Marcus was going to talk to you then go to the clinic. Martha said he wasn't there yet so I just need to verify he's with you."

Marcy was confused. "No, Helen. He came here, but I sent him back to class. He said earlier he wasn't feeling well, but we had a bad evening last night. I thought he was just out of sorts. Did they check the restroom? I'll come down to your office."

"I'll send someone to check right away, Marcy."

Helen called her custodian, who checked all the restrooms. Marcus was not to be found.

By the time Marcy reached the office, Helen already sent the custodian, and their security guard, back out to look for Marcus.

The secretary also called Principal Baylor, who was now reading to one of the first grade classes.

Marcy's face grew pale. "What could have happened to Marcus?" she asked with a crackling voice. "He's changed so much since Tim died. I never know what's going to happen next. Maybe he went out to our car. He should know it's too cold there though."

Marcy hurried back through the cafeteria to go out to her car. But there was no Marcus— and no footprints in the snow.

Several minutes passed, and everyone reported back to the office. There was no sign of Marcus, inside or out.

Marcy decided to call Lynn at home to see if she knew anything. "I can't imagine Marcus trying to walk home today. Maybe he called Lynn to pick him up and didn't tell me. She would check with me first though." Marcy rattled all of this off while Principal Baylor was reporting to the school superintendent concerning Marcus and trying to get a sense of the impending storm at the same time.

When Marcy hung up the phone, she burst into tears. "No one has seen him at home. My brother-in-law is going to drive around looking for him. I can't imagine him running away."

Helen parked beside Marcy with her arm around Marcy's shoulder. Quietly, under her breath, Helen whispered a prayer in Marcy's ear for Marcus's safety. Marcy knew Helen was a strong believer in prayer. She often asked Helen for prayer through Tim's accident and death. But all Marcy could say in her heart was "Please not Marcus, God!"

The security guard and principal went into the principal's office next door to check the videos at each entrance of the building. They always guarded the entrances but rarely guarded the cafeteria door since no one but the workers used that door.

Brittney Kennedy in her fifth grade class tried to act as normally as possible, but she felt like she ate a brick for breakfast. Helen's last call left her unsettled, and she knew something was wrong. She finished her math lesson and gave her students work that she hoped would last a few minutes.

"You may work together on this page. Please help each other until everyone gets these problems right." She hoped this would distract them as she called Charlie to the front to talk to him.

"Charlie, I know you and Marcus are good friends. What did he say to you this morning about coming to class?" Miss Kennedy inquired.

"Just what I said earlier. Marcus said his stomach hurt and he was going to ask his mom if he could go to the nurse."

"Are you sure that's all he said?"

"Yeah. Why? Is something wrong with Marcus?" Charlie asked, concerned.

"He's OK," Miss Kennedy replied, hoping it to be true. "Go back to work now."

The security guard stepped back into Helen's office. "Mrs. Hammond, come look at this please," he asked. "Someone exited the cafeteria door. The person was about the size of Marcus. What do you think?" he asked Marcy.

Marcy knew it was Marcus.

Principal Baylor was just trying to decide whether to put the school on official lock down because of Marcus or send students home because of the storm. Now that he knew Marcus had run out on his own, he had the security guard call the police. They soon discovered, however, that all footprints had been covered with the blowing, substantial snow. The principal called the school superintendent to update him on Marcus and make arrangements to send students home.

Marcy jumped to her feet. She had to search for her son herself.

Charlie. Get Charlie. She felt this strong impression as if she heard the words.

"Can we talk to Charlie Taylor, Helen?" Marcy urged.

"Sure. You think he knows something?"

Helen called Miss Kennedy's classroom again, and soon Charlie was in the office.

Now Charlie knew something was wrong. "Where's Marcus?" he asked.

"That's what we hope you can tell us. Has he said anything to you about leaving school to go home or anything else?" Marcy got right to the point.

"No, Mrs. Hammond. He's never talked about leaving, just coming to see you."

"No one's seen him since he left the cafeteria, Charlie."

Charlie replied, "Mrs. Hammond, he just said he was going to tell you his stomach hurt. And that's the truth."

Marcy replied, "He came to me, and I sent him back to class. We thought maybe he tried to go home, but he's not there. Do you think he would go to your house ?"

"Well, I don't know, but Mom was going to my grandma's today to help her clean, but maybe she didn't go because of the weather."

"Can you call your mom's cell phone and ask if she saw Marcus any time?"

Helen handed Charlie the phone; he talked to his mom right away. She had not seen Marcus. Now Charlie was afraid.

The security guard said that police were on alert and no one had seen any kids out of school at this point in time.

Meanwhile, Lynn called to say John was driving back and forth between home and school, but there was no sign of Marcus yet.

Marcy sat hard on the office bench with her head in her hands.

Charlie sat silently for a long moment weighing the possibility of Marcus going to their secret hiding place. If he told, he and Marcus would both be grounded for *life*. If he didn't tell and Marcus went there, Marcus might be trapped in the storm.

"Mrs. Hammond, Marcus goes down and hides at the old glass factory when he's upset. That's where he was the other day when you thought he was at my house. It's like a cool clubhouse under the loading docks that no one knows is there. Maybe he went there."

Marcy jumped up and hugged Charlie so hard he nearly fell off the bench.

"Thank you, Charlie. Oh thank you!"

She was on the phone to her brother-in-law instantly. "John, I know where to look! Meet me at the old glass factory on the loading dock side."

Principal Baylor was making an announcement that school would be closing early, but Marcy was already out and ahead of the buses.

The ice under the snow on the roads was prohibiting Marcy from driving as fast as she wanted.

John made it to the old glass factory first. It was only about a mile from home where he was then heading. The brown, fall growth around the building had already become icy and white. The snow made the sagging metal roof and broken windows look less forlorn. John pulled to the side of the road where the railroad passed the building. It was near the loading docks, but the area was overgrown with weeds and small trees. Marcy pulled her car up behind John's car just a few minutes later. John, with Marcy on his heels, trudged through the brush and snow.

"I don't see any footprints here, John. Why would he come here?" Marcy asked, not really caring for an answer.

The snow was falling thickly, and the wind was howling, whistling in the brush. Marcy's work shoes helped her in snow and ice, but she fell in a hole and was covered with snow. John pulled her up, and she trekked on, determined to find her son.

"Marcus! Marcus!" they both yelled intermittently. Surely he would hear them even in the howling wind since they were close to the loading docks.

They looked under dock number one—no Marcus. The wind whipped around stinging their faces with icy snow.

Dock number two—no Marcus

"Marcus Timothy Hammond, can you hear me?" Marcy screamed desperately.

Dock number three—no Marcus!

"I thought for sure he would be here!" Marcy yelled against the wind.

Suddenly, a creature bounded out from the shadows under the fourth dock. It was the old tabby cat, and Marcy jumped back and screamed from surprise.

John looked back under the dock, and there was something in the shadow. There was a big lump, too big to be another animal, and blood on the ground.

John suddenly disappeared then yelled, "Marcy, it's Marcus! He's alive but not awake! Call 9 1 1!"

Marcy was shaking. She called and tried to give their location as calmly as possible while she was crying.

John, kneeling by Marcus, knew he should not move him. Marcy crawled under the dock on her hands and knees. Even in the dim light, she could see the blood on the ground and feared what she would see. Marcus's head was gashed. She kissed him and cried.

"Marcy, go out and wait for the ambulance," John urged.

She would not leave the boy's side and kept whispering, "Please, God, don't let him die. Please, God!"

John climbed out from under the dock and ran back toward the car, waiting for the ambulance. Marcy hovered over her son, shielding him from the cold. She remembered the verse in Psalm 57:1 that she clung to when Tim had died. "In the shadow of thy wings will I make my refuge, until these calamities be overpast." Her tears dropped and froze on the ground.

It seemed like an eternity before Marcy heard the ambulance getting near. John guided the EMTs to the fourth dock and helped them pull Marcus out as they instructed. Soon John and Marcy were following the ambulance and calling Lynn and the school to let everyone know they found Marcus. The treacherous roads prevented them from getting to the hospital at top speed, but they passed several school buses taking children home because of the winter storm.

Marcy found herself in an all too familiar hospital room sitting beside Marcus's bed. She stared at the heart monitor waiting for test results and for Marcus to awake. John had gone out in the hall to call Lynn with an update and check on Gracie for Marcy. It had only been three months since Marcy sat in another hospital room with Tim, and anguish came over her.

"Please, God. I can't do this again. Please let him be all right!" Marcy prayed.

The emergency room doctor pushed back the curtain.

"Mrs. Hammond, Marcus does have a serious concussion, but we do not see any excess bleeding. He seems to respond to the pin pricks I tried, but we won't know the complete extent until he wakes up. We're going to take the bandages off his head and stitch him up now."

Marcy took a deep breath.

"We don't know how long he will be in the coma. A coma is the brain's way of protecting itself from the trauma that occurred. He may wake up in an hour or it could be a couple of days. We will be admitting him here soon."

John came back into the room.

"They're admitting him, John," Marcy said. "You need to go home before you're stuck here. They said it's a concussion but didn't find any major bleeding."

"Thank God!" John said. "Lynn and Gracie are fine at home. We have plenty of food there, and Lynn can keep Gracie busy. Lynn wants me to stay with you." He hugged his sister-in-law, knowing she really would be glad to have someone near. "When they get him situated in a room I'll go downstairs to get us some food."

"Thanks, John. You and Lynn are too good to me."

"We're family, kid," John answered.

They had all drawn close through Tim's accident and death.

Marcus was placed in the pediatric ward, and John retrieved paninis and fries from the cafeteria after Marcus was situated. John didn't know hospital food could be so good, but it tasted like a feast. He then went down to the lounge to rest and give Marcy some alone time with Marcus.

It was getting late. Marcy pushed the high-backed vinyl chair over to Marcus's bed. The monitor was showing steady vitals. Marcy covered herself with the extra blanket from the closet and propped her feet on the end of Marcus's bed.

The darkness draped a curtain of gloom over the hospital room and Marcy was feeling fearful again. *"What time I am afraid, I will trust in thee. Psalm 56:3,"* she recited over and over in her head. She was glad she had learned this years ago in Sunday school. "Dear God, help us." She said aloud.

Marcy's eyes grew heavy, but she felt too unsettled to sleep. The *drip, drip, drip* of the intravenous bag seemed loud to her. *Drip, drip, drip.* Tim was at the door! No, it couldn't be. She opened her eyes. No one was there. *Drip, drip, drip.* Tim was in the bed, and then he was gone. She shuddered. Now Marcus was on the ground with blood on his head. She gasped and jerked. She opened her eyes again. Marcus was there beside her in the bed. The monitor's lines were steadily moving as they should be. He was breathing OK and his heart beats were regular. His blood pressure was decent.

"Wake up, Marcus. Please wake up," Marcy whispered.

Suddenly it was 3:00 a.m. She must have dozed again, but she thought John was there touching her shoulder. As she opened her eyes, she saw no one but Marcus, but she felt a wonderful sense of relief and peace.

Then in the darkness, a whisper said, "I'm hungry."

"Marcus, is that you? Marcus?"

"Sure, Mom. I'm hungry."

"Thank you, God! Oh, thank you," Marcy cried as she called in the nurses.

As two nurses hurried past the lounge toward Marcus's room, John noticed and followed.

"He's awake, and he's hungry!" Marcy laughed as they all entered his room.

"Thank you, God," John said.

"Wonderful," said one nurse.

"It's about time!" declared the other.

Marcy and John stood at the foot of the bed while the

nurses attended to Marcus, and they called the dining service for pudding and ice cream.

John could not wait to tell Lynn that God had heard their prayers. He called Lynn right away and exclaimed, "Good news! Good news!"

Thanksgiving was bittersweet with Tim's empty place at the table. But Marcus's remarkable recovery had allowed him to eat his share of turkey and pumpkin pie. They celebrated by clearing the table to set up Marcus's remaining train so they could decorate it for the holidays, placing cotton around the tracks for snow.

Three weeks later, Marcus came bounding out of the church after the Christmas choir program. The snow crunched with his footsteps while it sparkled in the moonlight. Marcus's breath made clouds above his head, yet the air was still. He ran over to the Nativity scene where the infant was still sleeping peacefully. He knelt by the manger and said a prayer of thanks to the Christ who knew how he felt. Marcus now knew God loved him.

Soon crowds of people were exiting the church.

"Hey, Charlie!" Marcus yelled, hopping up with a spring. "Did you hear what Mr. Robinson told my mom? He said I could volunteer in his store after school every day after Christmas break. If I work really hard, he'll give my mom a discount on the train for my birthday."

Marcy and Gracie, holding hands, caught up with Marcus and headed for the car. Gracie grabbed Marcus's hand, and her brother did not resist as he normally did.

They stopped at the Nativity scene as the moonlight fell across the manger. A silence filled the air. This silence was filled with new hope and courage for the entire family.

This new hope and courage were born with the *real baby in the hay* that first Christmas night!

Crooked Foot

The brothers were standing on the grassy hillside dotted with rocks and watching the sheep lazily munch on grass.

Nathaniel flicked younger Simeon on the head.

"You can't kill a lion like David!" Nathaniel emphasized. "David was a great warrior and stronger than you'll ever be. I'm stronger than you'll ever be."

"Don't you remember I got a wild dog off mother's favorite lamb? That was when I was twelve. I'm fifteen now. I know I could kill a lion!" growled Simeon.

"I've been shepherding since I was seven and you think you have experience?" questioned Nathaniel.

"I don't know which of you can brag the most," their older brother Jacob scolded. "You're both worthless!"

Nathaniel dared Simeon. "Let's see if you can even get me down, *Crooked Foot*. I bet you can't even pin me, you swine!"

Simeon threw down his crutch and jumped on Nathaniel. The young men wrestled down the hill into the middle of bleating sheep.

Jacob ran to them and pulled them apart. "Now see what you've done? You're stirring up the sheep again. We were just getting them settled for the night."

The sun's last glow on the top of the acacia trees reflected the fluorescent orange linings of purple-gray clouds. The first star of the night appeared in the dimming sky, and fluttering bats flew haphazardly overhead. The brothers along with their cousin, Jeb, had wandered purposely toward Bethlehem this week as their fields were getting sparse. Their provisions were holding them as they planned, but they needed to head back home tomorrow. Jacob laid a pile of twigs and grass in the middle of last night's campfire ashes. He began striking two stones together to create a spark.

"You heathens go find some wood. We need to settle in and calm down."

Simeon picked up his crutch and hobbled to the thicket where he picked up twigs and broke dry brush off of shrubs. He was sick of Nathaniel calling him Crooked Foot and telling him he was incapable of handling himself. Nathaniel was such a boastful young man.

"I know more than them about sheep," Nathaniel would tell Simeon when Jacob and Jeb weren't in earshot. "I know as much as Jacob about what Father wants us to do with the sheep, and I'm always right, aren't I, Simeon?"

Simeon never answered Nathaniel. Maybe Nathaniel automatically thought Simeon agreed. *If Nathaniel says he knows more than anyone one more time, I'm gonna haul off and punch him,* Simeon thought.

Simeon took his sticks back to Jacob. "That's a small lot. It will barely get the fire started," growled Jacob.

Simeon couldn't even win with Jacob.

"I'm gonna get more. You know I can only carry so much using one arm!"

Simeon limped away on his crutch.

He remembered the day when the donkey stepped on his leg. His leg was so broken that it bent sideways. It hurt so badly

29

that he was in bed for weeks; his parents wrapped his leg tightly for months. At one point, they thought he'd lose his leg, so his parents sent for the healer from the next village. The doctor could do nothing more than they had done. He told them just to pray for a miracle. Now years later with a crippled ankle and no strength, he had learned to run with his crutch if he needed. Their mother said it was a true miracle that he even lived. She kept him from going out with the flocks until Father persuaded her that he needed to learn the family trade. Everyone knew Mother babied Simeon, but that wasn't his fault.

Simeon gathered more twigs and brought them to the others standing around Jacob. Jeb dragged up a dead tree branch from the bottom of the hill. It wasn't cool enough for a big fire tonight, but Jeb caught a couple of rabbits, and they were all looking forward to roasting them for supper. Besides, fires always kept the coyotes away.

"What's going on in Bethlehem?" Simeon asked. "I saw people on the far road all day."

"Where were you when we were talking about that earlier? They're registering for the Roman census. Each person has to register their household in their family town. Father will be going to Beersheba to register for the Roman census as soon as we get home," said Jacob.

The rabbits were cleaned and placed on the fire as the young men spread out their blankets and gathered breads from their satchels. Jacob's blanket was new. Mother had just made it out of her finest wool for his birthday.

"We'll save the cheeses for tomorrow," Jacob insisted. "Rabbit and bread will be a feast for tonight. We'll have enough other food to get us home."

A myriad of stars were now dancing in the clear, dark sky.

The absent moon allowed the stars to show off. The sheep were settled and sleeping for the most part, yet soft rustles and *baaas* were heard here and there.

"So why do we have to be counted?" Simeon asked.

"Think about it. If you were Caesar, you would want to know how many people you could tax!" Nathaniel scolded.

"If I were Caesar, you'd be gone," Simeon responded.

Nathaniel jumped up, and Jacob pushed him back down with a stare that was riveting even in the dark.

"Can't you boneheads be civil for an hour?" Jacob asked. "Be quiet, eat, and go to sleep. I'll take the first watch. It will be the only peace I've had all day!"

The next several minutes were silent. Not even the sheep made sounds. Then as a coyote howled in the distance, the small talk began again until the meat and bread were devoured. Everyone rested back on their blankets in the cool night breeze.

Simeon loved the stars. He remembered his grandfather telling him that God told the patriarch Abraham to count the stars, and that number would be the number of Abraham's descendants. Abraham was the father of their nation, and the father of their faith. Abraham was called "God's friend." Simeon wanted to be God's friend. Simeon knew that even with his disability, God would love him. Mother had always told Simeon so. The stars always reminded Simeon of Father Abraham and God.

Simeon lay back unable to sleep, so he tried counting the stars. They had already counted the sheep before they settled in for the night. *I guess an emperor would want to count his people*, Simeon thought. The others appeared to be sleeping.

Jeb was snoring, and Jacob, who was supposed to be on watch, had dozed off.

Suddenly, in the middle of the stars, a brilliant light shone down on the shepherds.

Simeon and the sleeping shepherds sat straight up, alarmed. They could not understand what they were seeing. They had heard stories of lands far north where colors in the sky would dance in the fall, but this wasn't *that*. They had seen shows of lightning on stormy nights, but this wasn't lightning.

A figure in the light spoke.

"Greetings, men. Don't be afraid! We have excellent news of joy for all people!"

The brothers and Jeb looked at each other with jaws dropped as if to say, "Are you seeing what I'm seeing?"

A glowing form, something like a person but not as defined, floated in the sky above them. The entire landscape was like daylight, and the wakened sheep looked as if they were stunned too.

"Today, in the town of Bethlehem, the City of David, your Savior was born!" the being exclaimed. "He is Christ the Lord, the Redeemer, the Messiah! Go to Bethlehem, and you will find the baby wrapped in cloths, lying in a feed trough in a stable because there was no room in the inn."

While the shepherds were staring in amazement, a massive army of bright beings surrounded the main messenger and began singing praises to the God of heaven and singing about *peace on earth* and *glory to God*. The shepherds had never heard any sound so beautiful and mesmerizing. It was an explosion of sight and sounds, and the shepherds sat frozen in their places.

Then, just as suddenly as the angels appeared, they were gone, leaving the shepherds and sheep under the starlit sky.

Jacob was silent.

Nathaniel said, "What just happened?"

Simeon thought he might have been dreaming, but the others were standing around dumbfounded just like he was. There wasn't anything to do but go to Bethlehem and look for a baby sleeping in a manger—of all things. He said, "We've got to go down there to Bethlehem. We've got to see if what the angels talked about is true."

Jacob shook his head. "Angels... Angels?"

Jeb was silent but standing, ready to go.

"What about the sheep?" Nathaniel asked.

"I guess we can let them follow to the edge of town then one of us can go ahead and see if we can find the baby," Jacob said. "You said *angels*, didn't you, Simeon?"

They gathered their staffs and satchels, laced their sandals, and were on their way. They followed the road toward Bethlehem, but it took them about twenty minutes to reach the edge of town.

Simeon knew the routine. His brothers and cousin would lead the way, and he would end up at the back of the flock because he could not keep up. It was usually fine with him because he would check on all the stragglers at the back. He knew how it was to be slow, but he didn't like anyone telling him that he was slow. But this time, he was excited, anxious, and curious to see what this was all about.

Nathaniel, Jacob, and Jeb were moving pretty fast. The sheep were good followers and moved along. Simeon was limping along as fast as he could. At one point, Jeb held back to check on Simeon, but Simeon was so excited that before long, he nearly caught up with the others.

They came along side night travelers going into Bethlehem. A stranger called to the shepherds. "What are you doing along this road? I think this road is for people."

"Even in this light, one of your friends looks like a donkey," Nathaniel called back.

"Donkeys can be family sometimes, mister," the man replied, laughing.

"Indeed!" yelled Nathaniel, looking back at Simeon.

For a while, the shepherds walked beside the travelers on the road; their sheep and Simeon followed. Then they let the travelers go ahead and slowed a bit to gather their sheep as they neared the edge of town. The sheep were all safely together as Simeon had kept a close watch.

"I'll stay with the sheep," Simeon offered. "I can handle it."

Jeb insisted he stay with Simeon while Nathaniel and Jacob went in search of the baby.

Several homes on the edge of town were dark and shut up for the night. No stables were lit or had anyone standing around. The blacksmith's barn had a couple of lanterns still lit. Someone was inside.

Jacob walked up to the door. A man was dousing a fire and hanging tools on the wall. Jacob didn't want to mention seeing angels; the man would think he was out of his mind.

"Sir, where is your town's inn?" He figured the inn must have a stable near it since the angel mentioned the crowded inn.

"I heard earlier today that it's full. You're too late and out of luck," the blacksmith blurted matter-of-factly, turning to check everything he had just put away.

"Can you tell me where it is anyway? We don't need to stay; we're looking for someone," Jacob firmly replied.

"You smell and look like shepherds. Who would you want?" asked the irritated blacksmith.

Jacob tried to calm his reply. "You are correct, but can you tell us where it is anyway? And by the way, you smell like a blacksmith!"

"All right, all right. Go four houses down, turn right, and it's on the hill there."

"That's all we need," Jacob replied while he hurried off trying to control his frustration.

Nathaniel ran ahead of Jacob and rounded the corner. They saw a large house on the hill. "That must be it!" Nathaniel yelled.

They saw people with lanterns walking the path beside it to a stable dug out of the stony hillside. There seemed to be a commotion, and indeed they heard a baby crying.

Nathaniel walked over to a lady standing at the stable doors and holding a lantern. "Was the Messiah actually born in this stable?" Nathaniel asked.

"Messiah?" the woman questioned. "I just helped this mother deliver her child here two hours ago. This is certainly not a wealthy couple. Messiah?" She snickered.

Another woman standing nearby broke into the conversation.

"The inn was full. This couple asked to stay in the stable because she was about to deliver. I've never seen anything like this happen in this town before. A baby born in a stable!"

"The angels told us to come to Bethlehem to see a newborn king. So here we are!" Nathaniel blurted.

"Angels?" The woman with the lantern snickered again.

The other woman looked at the shepherds then went inside to talk to the young mother.

"The mother wants you to come in," she said when she returned.

Nathaniel and Jacob walked cautiously toward the couple at the back of the stable. Two donkeys and a goat were in stalls at the side, and in a corner spread with fresh straw was the young woman lying beside a feedbox filled with hay. She looked to be a teen, with a simple, wrinkled tunic, but her face was radiant with the sweetest smile. The young man standing beside her was neither handsome nor plain but seemed to be proud of the newborn lying inside the feedbox. The teary eyed newborn was swaddled neatly in strips of linen. In the flickering shadows of the lantern hung near the baby, the young man was offering the young mother a drink from a goatskin canteen.

Nathaniel and Jacob stood dumbfounded. It was exactly as the angels had said. It took Jacob a couple of minutes to find his words. "We were lying on the hillside asleep by our sheep when we were awakened by what our little brother called an angel."

"He was glowing and white," Nathaniel chimed in. "He told us that a Savior was born today in David's city."

Jacob continued. "He said we would find a baby in a manger, wrapped tightly in cloths. Here he is just like the angel said!"

"Then they sang—a whole army of angels! It lit up the sky. We thought we were dreaming!" Nathaniel added enthusiastically.

The young woman began to cry as the man beside her knelt down to hug her.

The shepherds were not quite sure what was going on,

but the baby who had been crying earlier was now sleeping soundly in the hay.

The man beside the woman said, "I'm Joseph; this is Mary. We've both been visited by angels too. They told us to name him *Jesus*."

"We've got to go back to our brother and cousin," Jacob said. "May they come visit too?"

Mary nodded, and the shepherds hurried out. They thought it still seemed like a dream, but the whole thing was exciting.

The shepherds were quiet for half of their walk back to the flock. Nathaniel broke the silence first. "Why would a king be born in a stable? Why would he have a poor young couple for parents? I know that's what the angel said; we cannot deny it. Will anyone believe us?"

Jacob spoke authoritatively but thoughtfully. "Why would angels come tell us, shepherds, about a new king? The angel said he was born for us! A new king for the working man, *for all people!* His name is *Jesus*; *God saves!*"

Nathaniel was suddenly humbled in his heart. He always wanted everyone to know how good of a shepherd he was. He wanted to be better than his brothers. Better than Simeon, whom Mom spoiled. Better than Jacob, who was older and always seemed wiser. But there in that town, he had seen a baby who was supposed to be the King, the Messiah, the Savior, sleeping in a feed trough on a bed of hay.

He was anxious for Simeon and Jeb to see the baby.

The two older brothers ran the rest of the way back to the flock. Jacob decided he would stay with the flock on the edge of town while Nathaniel took the others to the baby.

"Wait," Jacob said. "Take my new blanket to the family. We also have an extra wedge of cheese and another loaf of bread we can spare. You need to take a gift."

Nathaniel looked at Jacob with humble understanding.

"Come on now, brothers. It's not too far, and you've got to see this baby," Nathaniel said in a matter-of-fact way. "Jeb, can you carry the supplies? Simeon, you can lean on me."

Simeon wanted to question if this was really Nathaniel. No criticisms or slams, just a helpful arm.

They made it rather quickly to the stable. Mary was now holding the young infant. He had just been fed and was sleeping in his mother's arms. The shepherds bowed before the baby. Joseph stood behind Mary with pride in his eyes. He was where God needed him to be, and the shepherds were the proof.

Nathaniel handed the blanket to Mary.

"This was Jacob's, my brother who was here earlier. It's new," he stammered. "And here are some extra bread and cheese," the boisterous shepherd said quietly.

Then Nathaniel handed the baby's father his own intricately carved staff. Nathaniel's grandfather had carved little sheep on the top third of the staff as a gift for Nathaniel when he began helping Father with the sheep. It was Nathaniel's favorite possession.

Simeon was in awe. The baby wrapped tightly in cloths was sleeping in his mother's arms, in a stable with smelly donkeys and a goat. And his loud brother was acting like someone he didn't know.

Jeb, always of few words, said quietly, "Praise the God of heaven and earth. It is all just as the angel said."

The shepherds left the stable quietly, not to wake the baby, but anyone out on the street that night heard the whole story from Nathaniel.

"There were angels—and a baby in the manger just like they said!"

Nathaniel even stopped at the blacksmith's house on the way out of town and woke him to tell him what they had seen.

That night, the shepherds were amazed that they had been visited by angels who told them about the baby king born in a stable. They hardly slept the rest of the night and started home with the sheep at the first glimpse of daylight. They were anxious to get home and tell Father about their news. They were amazed that the "Great I Am" would visit simple shepherds like he visited the patriarch Abraham and Moses himself, who was also a shepherd.

But something more had happened to them that changed them all that night. Nathaniel was humbled by seeing the child in the manger. He didn't need to prove to his brothers anymore how good of a shepherd he was. He stopped calling Simeon Crooked Foot and gave Simeon gentle instructions from time to time instead of criticizing him.

Simeon didn't have to prove that he could manage with a disability after that night. Although his foot was still deformed, his heart was healed, and his antagonism toward Nathaniel was gone. He somehow knew he was a valuable shepherd and lived with that conviction from that night on.

Jacob and Jeb knew in their hearts that the Messiah came for them—simple, stinky shepherds. And they were blessed to confirm the angel's message to the baby's parents.

Later that night, a bright star appeared in the sky as if it were shining down on only Bethlehem. Night after night for the longest time, it seemed brighter. The brothers and cousin often talked of that remarkable night on the hillside and told it to their children and grandchildren. They reminded their families of Father Abraham, the stars, and the brightest Star—the One born in a manger who came to heal hearts and relationships. And they remembered David's shepherd's Psalm and realized the Great Shepherd had come. He came for them. He was born in a barn of all places, and they were his first witnesses to the world!

For the actual Bible stories of Abraham, Moses, the shepherds, the star, and David's shepherd's Psalm, read the following:

> Genesis 15:1-6
> Exodus 3
> Luke 2:8-20
> Matthew 2:2-12
> Psalm 23

The Offering

Reuben's face was smudged and gritty. He smelled pretty gritty too. The clump of brush and fig trees at the city dump's edge was his summer home. His favorite time of year was fig season—the only time he had fresh fruit. He picked what he could at dawn before the neighbors came to find the trees. By then, he had already packed his satchel with fruit and picked up his tattered cloak that he used for a blanket. The fig season had ended, however, and a chill was settling into the air. He recently moved into a nearby cave where he'd spent the last two winters. Now he was having to search the trash dump for scraps of food, but they were few and far between.

These last two years were unthinkable. The picture of that frightening morning was still engrained on Reuben's mind. He was startled awake by his mother yelling at his father to wake up after Father had collapsed on the table. His little brother was screaming after the oil lamp had been knocked onto the rag rug, igniting it. Smoke filled the stone house, and his father was not responding. Before he could process all this, the thatched roof burst into flames and fell on his family as he jumped out the front door. He tried to get back in to help his family, but the flames and smoke were relentless. He fell in a heap alone on the ground, wailing, but no one lived near enough to know what was happening. By the time distant neighbors had come to check out the smoke from the fire, Reuben disappeared into the nearby cave out of fear. He was never discovered there. The town assumed the whole family was burned up in the smoking debris.

Reuben's first days alone were frightening. As a backward ten-year-old who knew no one in the city, he stayed in the cave. Their small field of grain had caught fire too, so he was hopeless without food. Finally, he remembered how his father found berries and dug roots, so he scrounged for what he could eat. He went for water a half mile away, where the stream was small and muddy. He barely survived but was ecstatic when he found the fig trees near the town dump.

But today was different for Reuben. He ventured past the figs and the dump and cautiously walked into the city market. He thought there was something special in the air, and indeed there was. The stench of extra camels and donkeys lingered in mid air, and the mass of people entering the city lent an even earthier mix of body odor and perfumes, creating a strange smell and excitement all at the same time.

"What's going on?" he asked the man walking alongside a wagon loaded with a woman and three children.

"It's a census, boy. Get out of our way. We need to get to the inn," grumbled the large man, who pushed him aside.

"What's a census?" he asked the man, ignoring his push but receiving no answer.

All day, Reuben watched the travelers coming into the town. Noticing the variety of strangers, he hoped to find a treasure or morsel of food dropped by the visitors. Today was his lucky day! He found a piece of bread he gobbled up in seconds, a small wooden dog, and a small, shiny coin. He was rich!

After careful inspection of the dog and coin, he stashed them in his satchel for safe keeping. The dog was the size of his outstretched hand, and its legs were on pins allowing them to move. It was even carved intricately with a coat resembling hair. It was the best wooden dog he had ever seen. And the coin—it was silver! *This coin*, he thought, *can buy fresh food at the market—maybe even a piece of fish!*

A sound brought Reuben out of his thoughts. Through the scuffle of donkey hooves and rattle of carts came the whimpering sound of a grown woman crying. Her tone was much like his mother's voice when his brother was born. Shuddering, he turned and saw a young woman sitting on a donkey. Reuben assumed the young man at the door of the nearby inn was her husband. Sadly, the man turned from the door with a bowed head, and after speaking to the young woman, he led the donkey behind the inn.

Somehow Reuben was drawn to this couple, and he wanted to know what was happening. He crept around the far side of the large building. He rounded the hill of the cave where the animals were kept. He listened for some time as the woman cried out intermittently. The young man hurried back and forth to the inn, finally bringing out a woman who carried a steaming kettle of water and a stack of cloths.

Soon there was the cry of a baby. Amazingly, Reuben had guessed correctly. The woman had her baby in a stable! Afraid he would miss something, he hung out in the nearby thicket, where he could see people come and go but he was not seen. Then, weary from his long but interesting day, Reuben fell asleep.

Sometime in the night, Reuben awoke, startled by men's voices, rustling footsteps, and bleating sheep. Peering from the bushes, he saw shepherds standing at the cave entrance. A strange light from above surrounded the stable, making their shapes rather clear, and the men were chattering all at once about angels, music, and a Savior.

Reuben crept out of the thicket and crouched down behind the shepherds near the little family. A flickering fire lit up the young woman's gentle face. She was smiling at the shepherds. The baby was gazing at his mother. He was snuggly wrapped in strips of cloth.

One shepherd took a blanket from around his shoulders and laid it at the woman's feet. Another reached in a satchel and gave the young couple bread and cheese wrapped in a cloth. Another shepherd left a staff with sheep carved in the handle. *This must be a special baby*, Reuben thought. *The shepherds left gifts for the family.*

Give him the coin, something said in his heart. *But I really would like a piece of fish,* Reuben reasoned.

Give him the coin, his heart said again.

He crept into the stable, hoping to not be seen, but the young mother smiled at him without speaking. He laid down the little wooden dog instead of the coin. He really wanted to keep the dog too. It was his first toy since his home burned. *Maybe the wooden dog will be enough of an offering,* he thought. But something still said, *Give him the coin!*

Reuben hurriedly handed the young man the coin and ran out of the stable, leaving both the dog and the coin. He ran to the edge of town and, with tears falling down his face, fell asleep again under a fig tree. He knew he had done the right thing, but he was heartbroken that his treasures were not his for long.

The bustling town was soon small and quiet again. The young couple with the baby disappeared, and Reuben's life was back to scrounging for food. He remembered that his father let people gather grain in the corner of his field and had instructed Reuben that God provided for the poor that way. Reuben learned where the good fields were, and he gathered unharvested grain for himself. He watched the farmers and went back to his cave, planting some of the grain nearby.

Year after year, he learned to survive and grew into a self-sufficient, young man. He learned to turn his loneliness into hard work. He gathered stones from the caves and fields and made himself a good shelter, then later a decent house. His patch of grain grew into a field, and he had enough grain to sell some to townspeople.

He found a sweet girl from the poor side of town, won her heart, and married her. They had three children, the oldest of whom was born blind. Reuben's tenacity kept him working through all of the hardships, and their family was as happy as any poor family could be.

One day Reuben and his wife, Lilah, heard of a healer who was staying in Jerusalem. Although their oldest child, Elizabeth, was blind, Reuben never considered her condition a hardship on the family. Lilah patiently taught her household skills, and Elizabeth fared well for an eight-year-old. Both parents still longed desperately for Elizabeth to be healed, and they wanted to find the famous healer who was often in Jerusalem.

Reuben and Lilah agreed that he would take Elizabeth to Jerusalem while Lilah stayed with the little ones. It would only take a couple of hours to get there if the trip went well, but if they couldn't find the healer right away, they were prepared. Reuben had materials to make a lean-to with the wagon, and they could spend one night.

The next day, packed with provisions and hope, Reuben and Elizabeth set out with their donkey and cart at dawn. The road was rocky and dry, but Elizabeth, taking all things in stride, encouraged her father that she was fine and having fun. She had never left their little town before.

As they neared the bustling city, the sounds and smells excited the child. She heard people chanting and children playing. She smelled bread baking and spices that were unfamiliar. As they neared the temple, she heard bleating sheep and mooing cattle; she smelled blood and cooking meat. Father described the great temple and the offerings given to God at the temple. Elizabeth was amazed.

They made it into the town and tied the donkey and cart near the cobbled city square. Reuben held onto his frail daughter as they walked around the market tables and carts.

"Have you seen the healer?" Reuben asked the first vendor.

"He was here yesterday. Haven't seen him today."

Reuben asked several vendors, who gave the same response. Finally, one vendor told him the healer was going back to Galilee and he'd probably left.

Reuben's heart sank.

Elizabeth said, "Let's go there, Father!"

"Too far, too far, child," he replied sorrowfully.

With a heavy heart, Reuben began to explain to his daughter that they would have to wait and find someone who would know when the healer might return.

Suddenly, around a corner came a group of chattering people. The leader was loud and grumbling.

"Leave him alone; he doesn't have time for them!"

The man in the center of the group who was surrounded by children reached out to the stern man. "It's fine. I'm delighted to see them. The kingdom of heaven is made up of children such as these. Don't ever discourage them. They are the innocent ones who know how to love and have faith."

The kind looking man in the middle of the crowd sat on a stone wall in the square, gathering the children around him and hugging each one.

Reuben picked up Elizabeth and carried her quickly to the man, being drawn with an unexplainable feeling. He put Elizabeth near the man. "Are you the healer?" Reuben interrupted.

The kind man returned with questions. "What do you need, sir? Is this beautiful child yours?"

"She cannot see, sir. We are looking for the famous healer."

The kind man slowly and sweetly patted Elizabeth on her head. Then with a gentle touch, he brushed his hand over Elizabeth's eyes, and she began blinking them.

Instantly she saw the gentle healer's face. She saw the beautiful blue sky. She saw the blue-green leaves rustling on the olive trees. She saw the bright, white limestone square. She saw the faces of other people and children.

Then she saw the face of her own father for the first time

as he swept her up. Elizabeth began calling, "Father, I can see! I can see!"

She put one hand on each side of Reuben's face and saw his sweet, large smile and his warm, happy, brown eyes.

Reuben spun around with Elizabeth in a dance of jubilation.

"Thank you, thank you, thank the God of heaven!" Reuben exclaimed.

They both hugged the healer, and Reuben asked what he required in payment.

"Just tell others what God has done," the kind man said.

Reuben bowed and thanked the healer again, and then he stood in awe.

The healer raised his hand to signal them to wait. He reached into the satchel the stern man was holding and pulled out something that he handed to Elizabeth. The little wooden dog was exactly as Reuben remembered.

Looking at Reuben, the healer said, "My parents told me about a boy who gave us this toy the night of my birth. My father and I replicated it in our carpenter shop. The boy also gave my parents a coin that helped pay for the sacrifice on the day of my dedication at the temple."

Tears streamed down Reuben's face. How could this be? He felt something he hadn't felt since he'd lost his family years ago in the fire. He now knew he was part of something—a plan, a design—he didn't really understand. It brought him and Elizabeth the healing they both needed, and the plan was completed by this man, God's Healer.

"Thank you, sir. Thank you!" was all Reuben could say.

Elizabeth, with great delight, gave the Healer another hug,

and the Healer was soon surrounded by more children and parents.

Reuben returned home that day hardly able to wait to tell Lilah all that happened. He had not only received healing for his precious daughter, but he had received healing for his painful childhood too. He knew years ago that he was to give his only treasures as an offering to that new born baby. And now he understood God saw his pain and remembered him! His family now had hope of a bright future!

He Came for Us

He came for us abandoning his glory—
no fanfare but to humble men who cared.
The angels sang to shepherds the great story,
while the world moved on quite simply, unaware.

In other lands, some scholars watched the heavens.
One brilliant light was beckoning to them.
They traveled far until they found their Savior;
with gifts and praise, they amply honored him.

How marvelous! The King of heaven's armies
gave his life to know us as his own!
And now, because he lives and reigns forever,
by grace and faith, we make our hearts his home!

This Tiny Human Baby's Hand

This tiny human baby's hand
once held the universe so grand
and by command created all things living.

So then, in compact human form,
He came to calm our raging storms
and teach us all to love and be forgiving.

No greater love was ever shown
that he would leave his glorious throne
so we can have a life that's now worth living!

Simple Thoughts

Christmas is for loved ones
gathered in one place
to celebrate God's blessings
and his wondrous gift of grace!

Christmas is a time of love
when people, blessed, will share
their gifts, their time, their hearts, their joy,
with those who need their care.

Christmas Bird

Little red bird in the tree,
sing your Christmas song to me
for hope has come and light has dawned—
and love's sweet song will carry on.

Christmas Rush

Amid the rush and bustle of another Christmas year,
did I throw out all my joy and love
for stress and doubt and fear?

Or-did I make each moment count and praise the Holy One
of whom this holiday proclaims
the greatest gift-God's Son?

As children we recited poems in church for special occasions. We called it "saying our pieces." I wrote this for my children's class to read for a Christmas program.

Did You See the Baby?

Did you see the baby sleeping in the hay?
He's the one who gives new HOPE for every passing day.

Did you see the baby in his mother's arms?
He's the one who brings us PEACE when others cause us harm.

Did you see the baby in the empty cattle stall?
He's the one who brings God's LOVE not just for one but all!

Did you hear the baby crying in the night?
He's the one who gives us JOY; He is the one true light!

He Lives—Eternal King!

Once long ago and far away,
a baby in a manger lay.
And though his cradle was not gold,
an angel choir, we are told,
proclaimed him to be King!

They sang the good news that dark night
to shepherds trembling with great fright
who could not wait to see the sight
and found the newborn King!

And though he grew to be a man
with humble ways he then began
to seek the hurting and the lost,
to love their souls at greatest cost,
then died not as a King!

Again the angels came to man
proclaiming him alive again!
His purpose was to conquer sin;
His mission was all souls to win!
He Lives—Eternal King!

In the Midst of Christmas Parties

In the midst of Christmas parties when commercialism reigns,
even Christians get involved in unnecessary things.

We shop; we bake; we carol; we party here and there
while we sometimes miss the lonely who need visitors and prayer.

And we sometimes miss the hungry or the homeless in the cold—
or the young and weary mothers, or the ailing and the old.

So at this special time of year, take time to share with others—
for it's the reason why Christ came—to help us live as brothers!

Christmas in Unsettled Times

The lights upon the Christmas tree reflect a sense of cheer.
They shine a peaceful glow to me in this unsettled year.

The light of Christ who came to earth can shine inside our hearts.
His mercy and forgiveness are the gifts his love imparts.

So celebrate this Christmas with the joy that Jesus brings!
For He alone can bring us peace; He is the One True King!

Let Us Rediscover Christmas

Let us rediscover Christmas
in this world that's dark and drear.
Let us hear the angel chorus;
let us feel the shepherds' cheer!

Let us see the new born baby
in the manger filled with hay.
Let us know he came for humankind
to give new life today!

Let us see him help the beggars,
and the grieving, and the lame.
Let us hear him say, "Forgive them,"
for that is why he came.

Let us rediscover Christmas
as we imitate Christ's ways—
for the light that shines at Christmas
needs to be in all our days!

n|m

About the Author

Nancy earned an accounting degree from Ball State University and worked in both the public sector and in the local public school system. She worked for the Muncie Community Schools in both the middle school and the administrative offices. Her true passion, however, is working in children's ministry which she has done for more than 30 years. Previously, she wrote children's activity books, poetry for church bulletins, and Sunday school curriculum for her church affiliate. She lives in Indiana with her husband, Roger, who is the music minister at their church. Nancy and Roger have two adult married children, and four grandchildren.

Printed in the United States
by Baker & Taylor Publisher Services